Matt and Mel's Mischief

Om KIDZ
An imprint of Om Books International

Om Kidz | Om Books International

Reprinted in 2023

Corporate & Editorial Office
A-12, Sector 64, Noida 201 301
Uttar Pradesh, India
Phone: +91 120 477 4100
Email: editorial@ombooks.com
Website: www.ombooksinternational.com

ISBN: 978-93-52760-29-9

Printed in India

10 9 8 7 6 5 4 3 2

Sales Office
107, Ansari Road, Darya Ganj
New Delhi 110 002, India
Phone: +91 11 4000 9000
Email: sales@ombooks.com
Website: www.ombooks.com

Matt and Mel's Mischief

Paste your photograph here

My name is

Matt and **Mel** are **merry** little twin boys.

They are very **much** alike.

They live with their **mother.** Their house is in the **middle** of a town called **Madison.**

It is in the lane between the **meat** shop and the dairy shop.

When their **mother** goes to the **market,** the boys are full of **mischief.**

They always keep **monkeying** around.

They love to play treasure hunt. They draw **maps** and **mark** the treasure on them.

They are even **more mischievous** around their **mother.**
"What is **my** name?" they ask as soon as she comes home.

Most of the time,
their **mother**
is correct.

Sometimes she **makes** a **mistake.** And then, **Matt** and **Mel** ask her to **make** their favourite **muffins.**

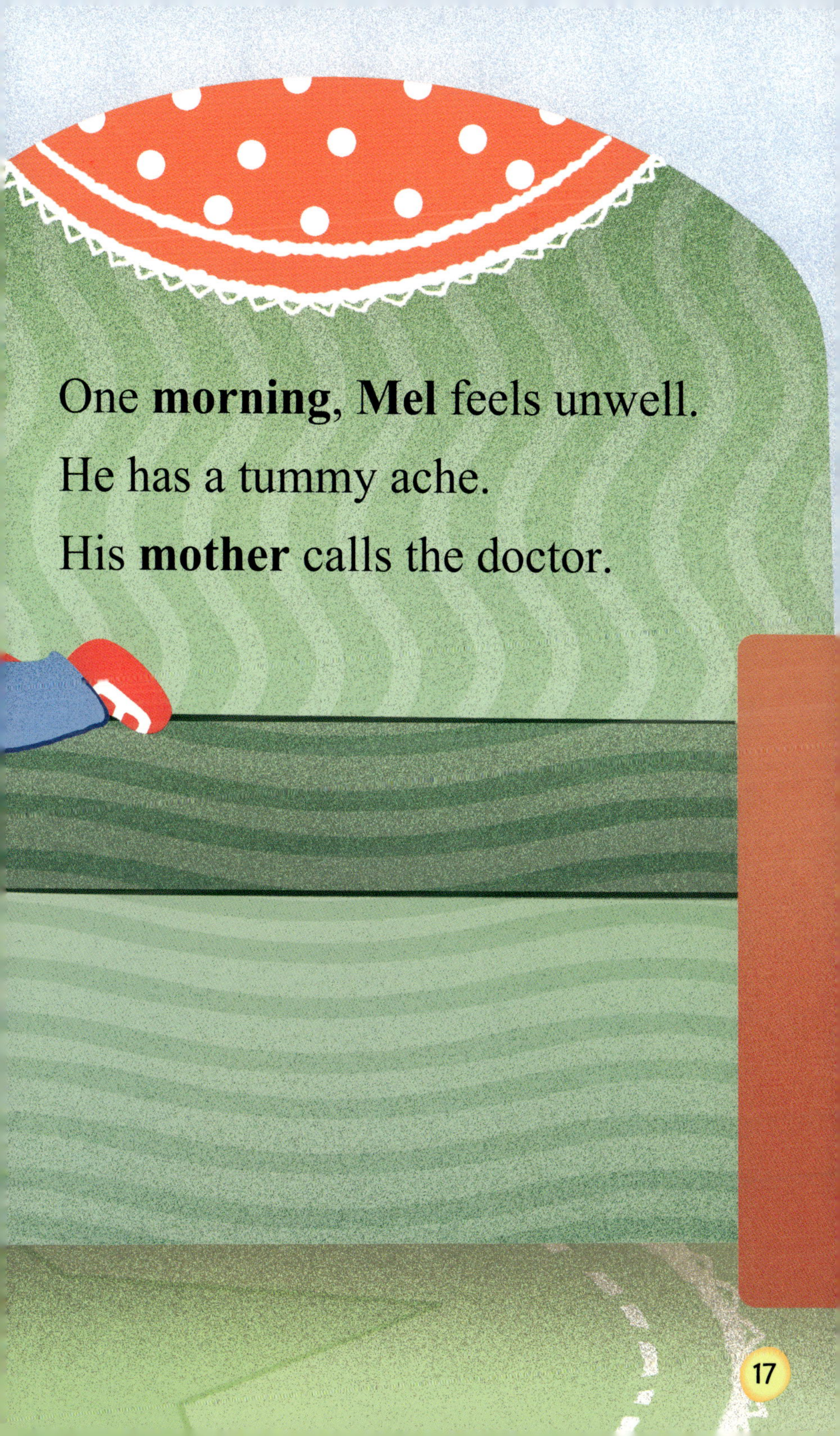

One **morning**, **Mel** feels unwell.

He has a tummy ache.

His **mother** calls the doctor.

The doctor is a tall **man.**

He **meets Mel** and checks him.

He gives **many medicines** for **Mel.**

After the **meal,** it is time for **Mel** to take his **medicines** but he doesn't like them at all.

Mel and **Matt** play a trick on their **mother.**

When she is not looking, **Matt moves** his table next to **Mel** and takes **Mel's** place.

Mother gives the **medicine** to **Matt.**

The **medicine** is very bitter.

Matt makes a face.

Mel misses taking the **medicine.**
His tummy keeps hurting.
Finally, both of them go and tell their **mother** what happened.

Their **mother** gives **Mel** his **medicine.** He **makes** a face too. **Matt** and **Mel** have now learned their lesson.

Know your words

Naming words

Matt	meat	morning
medicines	market	Mel
Madison	maps	man
mother	muffins	meal

Describing words

middle	many	merry
more		

Doing words

monkeying	makes	mark
misses	moves	

Sight words

mistake	much

Spot 5 differences between the two images.

Find the words in the word search. Use the clues given below.

I	W	M	I	L	K	Y	I
Y	M	E	D	C	N	Y	P
M	A	L	Z	A	R	C	N
E	R	M	A	N	Y	X	P
R	K	M	E	N	A	G	M
R	E	M	A	X	R	R	A
Y	T	V	N	R	K	A	K
G	B	Y	J	I	K	K	E

MILK MARK

MARKET MAKE

MERRY MANY

Circle the words starting with the letter '**m**'.

mistake	mother
trick	tummy
medicines	muffins
doctor	morning